The Ultimate Trainers

Paul Shipton

Illustrated by Judy Brown

Oxford

D1313071

Oxford University Press, Walton Street, Oxford OX2 6DP

Oxford New York
Athens Auckland Bangkok Bogota Bombay
Buenos Aires Calcutta Cape Town Dar es Salaam
Delhi Florence Hong Kong Istanbul Karachi
Kuala Lumpur Madras Madrid Melbourne
Mexico City Nairobi Paris Singapore
Taipei Tokyo Toronto

and associated companies in
Berlin Ibadan

Oxford is a trade mark of Oxford University Press

© Paul Shipton 1996
First published 1996
Reprinted 1997

ISBN 0 19 916915 2   School edition
ISBN 0 19 918518 2   Bookshop edition

Printed in Great Britain by Ebenezer Baylis

Illustrations by Judy Brown

The perfect trainers

Jake couldn't believe it when he saw them.

The trainers were on top of a cardboard box, next to a pile of rubbish bins.

Anna was busy telling him the plot of some science fiction book she was reading, but Jake wasn't listening. He just gazed at the trainers. They looked really good, and they looked brand new. At last he managed to speak, but only a single word.

Look.

Anna followed his pointing finger.

He edged closer.

But no – these were real, all right.

Anna was his best friend, but Jake didn't expect her to understand. She knew that he liked running and she even helped by timing him when he ran around the park. But Jake didn't just *like* running – he was *crazy* about it.

He peered inside the trainers.

They're my size too! Why would anyone throw them away?

Anna shrugged. Jake unzipped his school bag.

I'm taking them.

You can't just take them. They're not yours.

But they're being thrown away!

He could even hear the rumble of the dustbin lorry on its way from down the street.

You don't know where they've been.

It was Jake's turn to shrug. He stuffed the trainers into his bag.

'It's the Area Cross-Country Championships in two weeks,' he said. 'I'll never do well in my battered old trainers. These will give me a chance.'

Anna nodded. She knew how important the Championships were to Jake. Five runners were selected from each school in the area. Jake hadn't been chosen, but then Rob Curtis had gone to hospital to have his tonsils out. They picked Jake to be his replacement in the race.

Jake knew what the answer would be. They might be interested in different things – he loved running, and Anna spent all her time reading books about wizards and aliens and stuff like that – but he knew she would help him.

Kevin Beadle

Jake usually liked Thursdays at school, but that day seemed to drag on forever.

When the bell finally rang, he pelted to the changing rooms and got ready. The trainers felt fantastic on his feet – almost as if they had been made for him.

He was waiting for Anna outside the school, when Kevin Beadle walked by.

The bigger boy sneered when he saw Jake's gleaming new trainers.

Well, well. Slowcoach Jake has got himself some nice new trainers, eh?

Jake eyed him suspiciously.

That's right.

Beadle was the best runner in the school. The problem was that he *knew* it and he never let anyone else forget it either. Ever since Jake had joined the cross-country team, Kevin had been picking on him.

'They won't help, you know,' sneered Beadle. 'It doesn't matter if you run in snazzy trainers, flip-flops, or old army boots, Jake Crandall! The only thing you'll see of me in the Championships is a cloud of dust!'

He walked away laughing.

I'd like to wipe that smirk off his face, thought Jake. But he knew he had no chance of beating Beadle. He would be happy if he just did okay in the race – he didn't want to let himself down.

He looked up. Anna was coming this way, book in hand.

Jake tries them out

Anna sat on the park bench and got
her watch ready, while Jake did his
warm-up stretches.

I'll do four
laps today.

Anna nodded.

Okay. I'll tell you how
you're doing on each lap.

Jake began to run. Anna glanced at
her watch, then she opened her book
and started reading.

Usually Jake set out at a light jog at first. But today was different. He reached top speed straight away. He didn't plan it – it just happened. It felt as if he was running on air. His feet were a blur.

He had to shout to Anna so that she would look up from her book. She called out his lap time as he whizzed by. She couldn't believe he had finished one lap already.

That's your fastest ever!

But the second lap was faster yet. Jake zoomed round and he didn't even feel out of breath. Not at all! In fact, he felt wonderful. And he was still picking up speed!

Anna had stopped reading now. She was watching in amazement.

The third lap flashed by too. This was normally the time when Jake got a stitch in his side and his breath began to wheeze. Not today. He zoomed around the park and he still felt completely fresh.

It almost felt as if the trainers were doing the running for him and he was just along for the ride!

Anna didn't even check the watch now.

The fourth lap was the fastest of all.

Then there was the screech of rubber on concrete as Jake came to a stop.

Jake shook his head and grinned. But Anna just narrowed her eyes.

Jake looked down at the amazing new trainers. He was so excited that he did not notice the tone in Anna's voice, as if she thought that something was *very, very wrong here.*

Anna works it out

Jake decided to keep the trainers in his locker at school. He didn't want to take them home.

'My Mum and Dad'll never believe I found them in the rubbish,' he explained. 'They'll make me hand them in to Lost Property.'

The next day Jake decided to do six laps of the park. Anna made sure she was there again to watch.

Just like before, Jake set off at an amazing pace. Once again he was amazingly fast, and once again he wasn't out of breath at all. His feet flew over the ground and he finished the first three laps in lightning speed.

This time Anna watched carefully. She knew no pair of normal trainers could make such a difference. She tried to think of an explanation, but she couldn't.

She had read stories about things like magic rings and lanterns ... but that's just what they were – *stories*. And she had never heard of anything as weird as magic *trainers*!

Suddenly a dog charged out across Jake's path. Anna tried to shout out a warning, but she was too late.

Jake didn't seem to notice the dog, but he leapt into the air. He soared high over the puzzled dog, then went on running. He finished the lap and stopped when he reached Anna.

Understanding hit her like a bucket of cold water. It was crazy, but somehow she knew it was true.

'It's the trainers!' she burst out. 'It's like they have a life of their own! I mean, no one could run so fast. The trainers were doing it. You were just a passenger.'

Anna broke in, 'And just now …
somehow the trainers "saw" that dog.
Somehow they "knew" to jump over it.'

Anna's mind was racing. Trainers
that could think for themselves?
Magic? Aliens, maybe? They didn't
look very alien, though – they even
had MADE IN THE UK written on the
bottom.

21

She knelt down and stared straight at the trainers.

Of course, the trainers said nothing. But Jake was stepping back. He was angry.

'Listen!' he said loudly. 'I don't care what the trainers are, or where they came from! All I know is this – now that I've got them, I'm going to win the Area Championships!'

Anna shook her head. 'It won't be YOU who wins, will it? Anyone could win if they wore those trainers. It won't prove anything ...'

But Jake wouldn't listen.

'You think I should give them up, don't you?' he shouted. 'Well I won't! These trainers are my only chance to win that Championship. I don't need to know how they do it ... and I don't need any help!'

With that he turned and ran off like a speeding train.

'It won't prove anything'

The day of the Championships drew closer. Every day Jake went to the park to run, and every day he took the trainers back and carefully placed them in his locker.

He just wished Anna could see how fast he was now. He felt terrible about having a row with her. *But,* he told himself, *Anna just doesn't understand how important this is to me. I can make things up with her after the race. Better to concentrate on winning for now.*

And it seemed certain that he would win. How could he lose?

With each session he was even faster. He just had to relax and the trainers did the running. He didn't even have to move his arms. He could run along eating a bag of crisps or reading a comic and he was still as fast as ever.

Soon it was the Friday before the big race. Jake had his final training run around the park.

When he finished he checked his watch – it was his fastest time yet.

So why didn't he feel happy about it? Anna's words echoed in his mind: 'It won't be YOU who wins ... It won't prove anything ...'

Jake trudged back to school. He didn't even notice that someone had been watching him as he ran.

Someone who could not believe his eyes.

Someone who followed Jake all the way back to school, and watched him place the trainers in his locker ...

... Kevin Beadle.

Jake makes up his mind

Jake slept badly, but in the morning things seemed clear. He'd been so stupid! It wasn't worth falling out with Anna just to win a race.

Besides, he thought, she had been right – it wouldn't mean anything to win by using the trainers. *Anyone* could do it. No, he would run the race in his battered old trainers.

As soon as he'd made his mind up, he felt happier. He gobbled down breakfast and rushed over to Anna's house.

When she opened the door, Jake
looked his friend in the eye.

They grinned at each other and Jake
told her about his decision.

'I want to hand those trainers in
before the race even starts,' he said
firmly. 'That way, I can just
concentrate on my running.'

So the two of them dashed over to the school. No one was around yet, and it was quiet inside the school. They were hurrying along the corridor, when suddenly they noticed that something was wrong. It was Jake's locker. The lock had been snapped off. The door hung open and inside there were a few exercise books and a pencil case ... but no trainers.

And that's when they realized they were not alone. A voice behind them said, 'That's *my* question.'

Jake and Anna whirled around. They were face to face with two adults – a woman and a man. Where had *they* come from?

The first thing Jake noticed was how strangely they were dressed. They were both very tall. The woman was holding something which looked like a pocket calculator. It let out a low beep.

The woman smiled.

At first, Jake thought it must be some kind of joke. But that wouldn't explain the strange look on Anna's face …

31

With a jolt he realized – the woman
meant the future,
as in tomorrow,
    next week,
        next year,
            next …
But that couldn't be – it was
impossible!

And then he saw that the two adults
were not so tall after all. They were
hovering in the air just above the
ground.

They both clicked buttons on their
belts and floated gently to the ground.

Where are the trainers?

Anna looked calm. (Later Jake realized why: she had read so many science fiction books that she was prepared for this moment.)

The little man smiled.

Jake looked at the man's pot-belly. He didn't *look* much like an athlete.

In fact, Luther didn't look as if he could jog down the road without puffing and panting. He seemed to guess what Jake was thinking.

'In our time, sports are very different,' he explained. 'Athletes all design and build their own special running shoes. These trainers all have Artificial Intelligence circuits.'

'What does THAT mean?' asked Jake, feeling stupid. But Anna understood.

It means they do the running for you. They can even think for themselves when they need to.

Luther nodded. He went on, 'But this pair can think for themselves *too much* – they decided to run away. They went to a Time Travel Holiday Centre and they persuaded the computer there to send them back in time. To *your* time.'

'That's why we're here – to bring the trainers home,' said Mariah. 'It took us a while to track them down. We were unfamiliar with your primitive methods of transport.'

But finally we followed the trail to this place. Unfortunately we were too late.

She pointed to the open locker and sighed. She held up the beeping machine. Jake realized it must be for tracking the trainers.

According to my readings, they're somewhere outside.

BEEP

Jake nodded grimly.

And I bet I know who's got them.

The big race

The four of them hurried outside.

It was almost time for the big race. There were people everywhere, and there was a buzz of excitement in the air. Proud mums and dads were picking out the best places to watch the race.

Runners were warming up, pinning their numbers onto their vests, taking last minute advice. It wasn't hard to spot Kevin Beadle – he was the one with the smug look on his face. Jake could see why – he was wearing the trainers!

Mariah nodded, but it was clear that Luther had another idea. There was a twinkle in his eye.

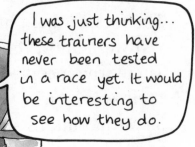

Mariah thought it over, then at last she agreed.

Luther nodded.

For a second, Jake felt a sharp stab of jealousy. Beadle was bound to win easily with those trainers. Then he remembered his own kit. It was almost time for the race to begin! With so much going on, he had forgotten to get changed.

I'll be back in a minute.

After he had changed, Jake was only just in time for the start of the race. The race organizer called the runners to the starting line.

Jake could see Kevin Beadle in the middle of the pack. A smirk played on the tall boy's face. Jake told himself to ignore it.

The whistle blew and the race began. Five laps of the school playing fields. Right away, Kevin Beadle sprinted to the front of the pack. The trainers were doing their stuff.

But Jake told himself just to concentrate on his own running. It was tough – he had spent so long running in the amazing trainers that real running was hard work.

After the first lap he was near the back, and his legs ached. He spotted Anna in the crowd. The two strange adults were still with her. Anna shouted to him.

C'mon, Jake! You can do it!

That made him feel better. He forced himself to go faster. Beadle, of course, was far ahead of all the other runners.

After the third lap, Jake was around the middle of the pack. His side was starting to hurt and his breath burned in his lungs, but he would not let himself slow down.

There was something good about
the way it felt. Whatever happened, it
was up to him, not the trainers.

Beadle increased his lead.
The fourth lap was the hardest yet.
It was the time when runners began to
puff and pant, and a lot slowed down.
But Jake gritted his teeth and pushed
on. He overtook a few runners. He
didn't even look up to see how far
ahead Kevin Beadle was.

And then he was passing Anna for the last time – it was the last lap. Even Luther and Mariah looked excited now. Luther was jumping up and down and yelling at the top of his voice.

The last lap was a blur. Jake's whole body ached, not just his legs. But on he ran.

Just when he thought he couldn't run another step, he heard a cheer from up ahead. Kevin Beadle had crossed the finishing line. The tall boy was holding up his arms.

That gave Jake an extra burst of energy. He dug deep into himself, and ran on for the finishing line. Other runners jostled elbows against him as they made their final charge for the finish as well.

At last Jake crossed the line. He was tenth – much better than he had expected!

He bent over and tried to catch his breath. He was exhausted, but he felt pleased with himself as well.

He looked over at the winner, who was standing with a group of admirers. Of course, Kevin Beadle looked as fresh as he had at the start of the race.

But Jake didn't even care any more. He knew that Beadle had not really won at all. *The trainers* had won for him.

Anna rushed over and gave Jake a great big hug.

You were great!

The trainers get their own back

Mariah and Luther came to join them. Luther slapped Jake on the back – he really seemed to like 'old-fashioned' running.

'Fantastic!' he said. 'I never knew running could be so exciting. But it looks like very hard work.'

That's the point of it. And next year I'm going to train really hard. I'm going to win the championships.

Well, we'd better collect the trainers and go home.

Wait! I still don't understand. What made the trainers run away to our time?

'They're a new design – the most intelligent trainers I ever designed,' Luther told them. 'They've even got basic emotions. But there's a problem with them. They're a bit moody and sometimes … sometimes they get angry. That's why they ran away.'

The calculator (that wasn't really a calculator) started beeping even louder. Mariah pointed it at Kevin Beadle, who was still boasting to anyone who would listen.

BEEP
BEEP
BEEP

She looked worried. 'Yes, and we'd better hurry,' she said. 'According to my readings, they're getting angry right now. That boy must be irritating them. If we're not quick –'

But she was too late.

One moment Beadle was bragging about how easy the race had been. Then suddenly the smirk disappeared from his face and he started jogging on the spot. It was clear that he couldn't stop. It was the trainers!

And then – ZOOOOOM! – Beadle charged off. As he raced away, everyone could hear him shouting.

But he did not stop. He jumped high over the school gates and raced along the pavement at top speed. He had no control over where the trainers were taking him.

The whole crowd at the finishing line stared in silent amazement. Jake and Anna watched along with everyone else. Kevin Beadle had zipped across the road, and now he was racing towards the petrol station.

It was true! Kevin Beadle sprinted through the car wash. When he came out at the other end he was soaked. A big dollop of foam perched on his head.

But still he did not stop. He didn't even slow down. He charged down the street, picking up speed, until at last he was just a small figure in the distance.

Back to whenever

It was an hour before the trainers returned, bringing a stunned Kevin Beadle with them. By that time everyone else had gone.

Beadle didn't ask any questions. He just pulled the trainers off and handed them over with a dazed look on his face. Then he staggered away in his socks.

Luther looked down at the trainers. Jake and Anna recognized that look in his eyes – happiness and relief, as if he had found a missing pet.

The trainers hopped up into his arms – whatever they had been angry about was forgotten.

Mariah began tapping the keys on another gadget in her hands.

(It sounded like she had a bus to catch, rather than a different time to go to.)

Luther leaned forward to Jake and spoke as one athlete to another.

And good luck in your next race.

The gadget in Mariah's hand beeped. Anna jumped forward.

Wait! There's so much more I want to ask!

But she was too late.

The two visitors disappeared in a flash of blue light – back to *whenever* they came from.

Anna and Jake were left alone. They just looked at each other.

Well, you don't see _that_ every day. It reminds me of this book I'm reading...

She pulled a book out of her pocket. It was called *Time Travellers of Zob*.

Jake pulled a face and Anna grinned. She pushed the book back into her pocket.

'You're right,' she said. 'I think I'm going to read a thriller next. I've had enough of time travel for a bit.'

About the author

When I was growing up
in Manchester, I always
wanted to be an
astronaut, a footballer,
or (if those didn't work
out for any reason)
perhaps a rock star. So it
came as something of
a shock when I became
first a teacher and then an editor
of educational books.

I have lived in Cambridge, Aylesbury, Oxford
and Istanbul. I'm still on the run and now live
in Chicago with my wife and family. I always
liked cross country running at school, and I
think this story may have been a daydream
of mine.

Other Treetops books at this level include:

I Wish, I Wish by Paul Shipton
The Personality Potion by Alan MacDonald
The Goalie's Secret by Paul Shipton
Waiting for Goldie by Susan Gates
The Case of the Smiling Shark by Tessa Krailing

Also available in packs
Stage 13 pack B   0 19 916918 7
Stage 13 class pack B   0 19 916919 5